CHRISTMAS MEMORIES

Family faces are magic mirrors.
Looking at people who belong to us
we see the past, present, & future.
♥ GAIL LUMET BUCKLEY

Our Book,

ISBN 0-316-10648-8

Published by Little, Brown and Company

BOSTON · NEW YORK · LONDON

For more information on homemade books
by Susan Branch, go to www.susanbranch.com
or write for my free newsletter to
Susan Branch
Box 2463
Vineyard Haven, MA 02568

10 9 8 7 6 5 4 3 2 1

PRINTED IN THE UNITED STATES OF AMERICA

Christmas Love

"h friends, dear friends, as
  years go on & heads get gray,
how fast the guests do go!
Touch hands, touch hands,
  with those that stay.
Strong  hands to weak,
  old hands to young,
Around the Christmas board
  touch hands. "

♥ Wm. H. H. Murray

HOLLY JOLLY CHRISTMAS

The little things that make life sweet
Are worth their weight in gold;
They can't be bought at any price
And neither are they sold. ♥

I've kept diaries for years, so all of my Christmases have been recorded. Some of my memories go into my little "PARTY" journal where I write about special dinners & parties ~ the food, music, guests, flowers & decorations. There are more Christmas memories in my everyday journal ~ & still more show up in my photo albums. But I started thinking, wouldn't it be wonderful to look at 5 years of Christmas all in one book? 5 years of family photos, 5 years of Christmas trees, Christmas Dinners & Christmas Eves; 5 years of memories by family members ~ signatures of the youngest, jokes by the oldest ~ visits to Santa, Christmas pageants, family toasts & prayers. Wouldn't you have loved it if your Great Grandma had done this for you!!? YES!

So here's your chance to make a family legacy. Just fill in the lines, use a glue stick to add in some photos & voilà ~ a book of memories to go down in family history. ♥ All yours, all original & all with love from the Heart of the Home & me...
Susan Branch

It's not that I belong to the past, but that the past belongs to me. ♥ Mary Antin

'TIS THE SEASON

WHEN YOU COME RIGHT DOWN TO IT, THE SECRET OF HAVING IT ALL IS BELIEVING THAT YOU DO.♥

IT'S THE LITTLE THINGS THAT MEAN THE MOST

A simple & beautiful seasonal decoration is a wooden bowl filled with evergreen boughs topped off with golden pears.

Candles are wonderful & romantic — they can also be cute at a party if you hollow out apples & plop in candles.

If you put boughs of holly, ivy, or boxwood — anything with a woody stem — in water, hit the cut end with a hammer first. It helps the water get to the leaves. ♡

MISTLETOE KISSES

Even tho' it's chilly — extra care should be spent to be outside admiring nature this month — staves off STRESS.

Sprinkle those shiny little gold stars over your tablecloth — makes magic!

Listen to your children — sometimes they'll be wanting to show their love when you are busy — take time to stop & return their love with special hugs & kisses.

Plan something special for January, a little trip or a party, so that all the focus isn't on the holidays & you can say, "Oh boy, I can't _wait_ for January."

Dress up your house ~ use bowls of pinecones, apples, pomegranates, cranberries, holly, cinnamon bundles, tangerines & lemons studded with cloves. Candy canes, candy houses, chocolate Kisses, poinsettias & mistletoe.

The best gifts are handmade ~ gifts of food, knitted, embroidered, or quilted things; wooden things & painted & drawn things ~ whatever you're good at. Encourage your children to be creative too. ♥

CHRISTMAS MORNING

Baked Apple

per person: 350° Makes your kitchen smell like heaven!

1 Tbsp. oats
½ Tbsp. brown sugar
½ Tbsp. chopped walnuts
2 tsp. soft butter
pinch of cinnamon

pinch of nutmeg
dash of lemon juice
1 Tbsp. apple juice
1 apple, Cortland or Rome Beauty

Preheat oven to 350°. Wash & core apple, being careful not to break through bottom. Mix together all the rest of ingredients except for apple juice. Fill the apple with the mixture & put it in a shallow baking dish. Pour the apple juice around the apple & bake for 25 min., till tender. Delicious with a splash of heavy cream.

♥ ♥ ♥

TRADITION: Do some things exactly the same every year ~ always give flannel jammies, have the same Christmas breakfast, or stop by a pastry shop for Chocolate Eclairs while shopping. It's the over & over again that makes memories that last forever ♥

Be an Elf

Make Magic

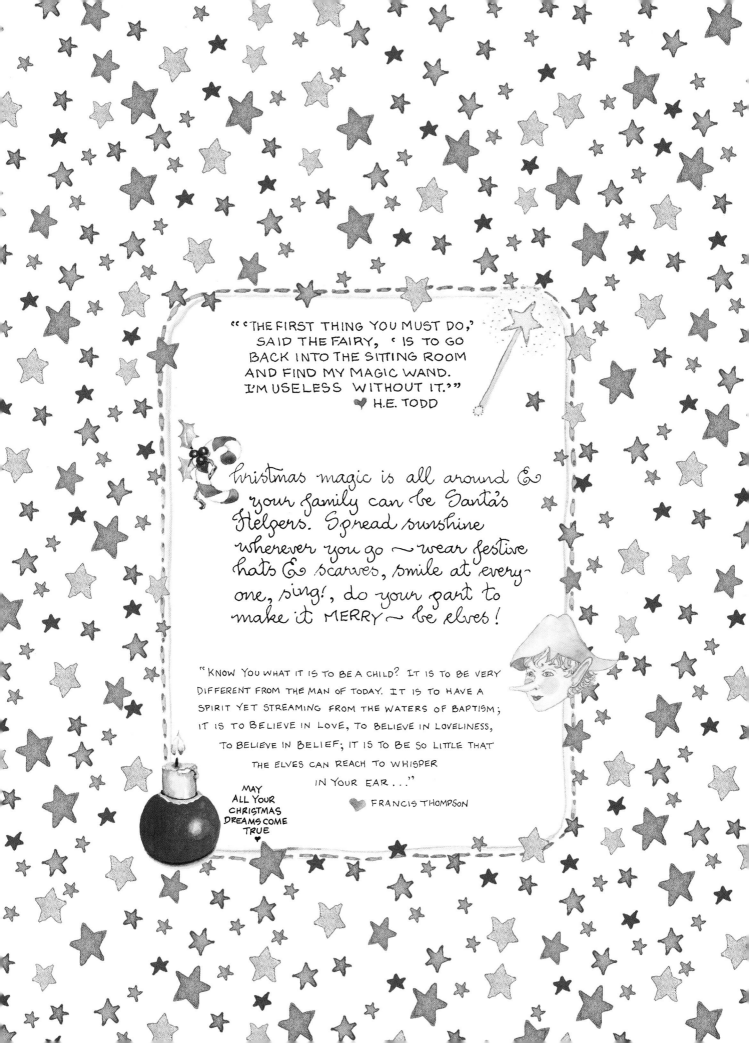

" 'THE FIRST THING YOU MUST DO,'
SAID THE FAIRY, ' IS TO GO
BACK INTO THE SITTING ROOM
AND FIND MY MAGIC WAND.
I'M USELESS WITHOUT IT.' "
♥ H.E. TODD

Christmas magic is all around &
your family can be Santa's
Helpers. Spread sunshine
wherever you go ~ wear festive
hats & scarves, smile at every-
one, sing!, do your part to
make it MERRY ~ be elves!

" KNOW YOU WHAT IT IS TO BE A CHILD? IT IS TO BE VERY
DIFFERENT FROM THE MAN OF TODAY. IT IS TO HAVE A
SPIRIT YET STREAMING FROM THE WATERS OF BAPTISM;
IT IS TO BELIEVE IN LOVE, TO BELIEVE IN LOVELINESS,
TO BELIEVE IN BELIEF; IT IS TO BE SO LITTLE THAT
THE ELVES CAN REACH TO WHISPER
IN YOUR EAR . . .' "
♥ FRANCIS THOMPSON

MAY
ALL YOUR
CHRISTMAS
DREAMS COME
TRUE
♥

COUNTING OUR BLESSINGS

A Prayer for a Little Home

God send us a little home;
To come back to when we roam.
Wooden floors & fluted tiles;
Wide windows, a view for miles.
Red firelight & deep chairs;
Small white beds upstairs.
Great talk in little nooks;
Soft colors, rows of books.

One picture on each wall;
Not many things at all.
God send us a little ground;
Tall trees stand 'round.
Homely flowers in fertile sod;
Overhead, thy stars, O God.
God bless thee when winds blow,
Our home and all we know.

Florence Bone

"And each heart is whispering
'Home, home at last!'"

Thomas Hood

Glue your family
Christmas card,
your dinner menu,
or favorite party
invitation here.

CHRISTMAS STAMP

Glue
Here

OUR FAMILY

GOD BLESS US EVERY ONE

CHAIN-CHAIN-CHAIN   CHAIN OF LOVE ♪

A Favorite Photo

Memories from the Year of _____

OUR
TRADITIONS

GETTING THE TREE, VISITING, HOLIDAY BAKING, HANGING THE STOCKINGS, EGGNOG

_____
_____
_____
_____
_____

Memories are made of this ♥ _____
_____
_____
_____
_____
_____
_____
_____
_____
_____

Our Favorite Christmas

Decorations ♪

Ornaments

Carols

Food

Drink

Smell

Book

Music ♫

Movie

Moments

Best Cookie:

Biggest Cookie Monster
THE AWARD GOES TO

Decking the Halls

How we decorated . . . inside & out . . .

. . . ♫ OH, THE WEATHER OUTSIDE ♪ IS FRIGHTFUL,

BUT ♫ THE FIRE IS SO DELIGHTFUL ♪ . . .

The Tree

How dear the memory is to me,
The lights, the fun,
the Christmas Tree. ♥

Dear Santa,

We've been soooo good ♥. We hope you'll bring us . . .

HO HO HO

CHRISTMAS IS FOR CHILDREN

PLACE A PHOTO HERE,
DEAR.

His eyes how they twinkled!
His dimples how merry!
His cheeks were like roses,
His nose like a cherry!

Noticing the
Little Things...

_____
_____
_____
_____

Something Funny
Happened...

CHRISTMAS BLOOPERS & PRACTICAL JOKES

WHAT FUN IT IS TO LAUGH & SING...

HOW'S THE WEATHER?

It's that time of year when
it's good to be
fat & jolly ♥

OH BY GOSH BY GOLLY

Favorite
Parties...

CELEBRATIONS

Festivities

TIME FOR MISTLETOE & HOLLY

Our Friends

"The simplest pleasures warm true friends most easily." *Alyson Roay*

PHOTO
HERE

A loving heart is the truest wisdom.
♥ CHARLES DICKENS

MISTLETOE KISSES

A JOY SHARED IS A JOY DOUBLED

The whole family has to sign their names — tell a joke, a story; tell about their favorite things; the family pet, new faces in the family — people we miss, places we love to go, how we share our good fortune.

_____

_____

_____

_____

_____

_____

_____

_____

_____

_____

_____

_____

_____

_____

_____

"For somehow, not only at Christmas, but all the long
year through, the joy that you give to others is
the joy that comes back to you."
♥ John Greenleaf Whittier

MERRY CHRISTMAS

Christmas Eve

Table, menu, guests, toasts, music, last~minute wrapping...

Snacks for Santa

'Twas The Night Before Christmas...

OH BY GOSH BY JINGLE

DARKNESS FALLS STARS APPEAR
EVENING ANGELS GATHER HERE

SWEET DREAMS

Backward, turn backward,
O Time in your flight;
Make me a child again
Just for tonight. ♥ Elizabeth Akers Allen

UNDER THE TREE

NO PEEKING

SHHHH

Best-Kept Secret...

The best gifts are tied with heartstrings.

MERRY CHRISTMAS

On Christmas Day...

HO HO HO

I heard the bells
on Christmas Day
The old familiar
carols play
of Peace on Earth
Good will to All.

Christmas Dinner
Guests • Menu • Flowers

_____

_____

_____

_____

_____

_____

_____

_____

_____

Our Christmas Prayer _____

_____

_____

Every act of love
is a work of peace
no matter how small.
♥ Mother Teresa

HOME
for CHRISTMAS

BLESSINGS

THERE'S NO PLACE LIKE HOME

TO US

HAPPY NEW YEAR

RING OUT THE OLD, RING IN THE NEW

We Brought in the New Year. . . .

AND CELEBRATED NEW YEAR'S DAY. . .

"**L**ost, yesterday, somewhere between sunrise and sunset, two golden hours, each set with sixty diamond minutes. No reward is offered, for they are gone forever."

♥ Horace Mann

We resolve...

★
★
★
★
★
★
★
★
★

Before you go to bed on December 31st, join hands, say a prayer, & make a wish for the coming year. It's been proven that, when lots of people pray at the same time, miracles can happen. "In this season it is well to reassert that the hope of mankind rests in faith. Believing there is hope for the world is a way to move toward it." ♥ Gladys Taber

FAITH

Glue your family
Christmas card,
your dinner menu,
or favorite party
invitation here.

CHRISTMAS STAMP

Glue
Here

OUR FAMILY

GOD BLESS US EVERY ONE

CHAIN~CHAIN~CHAIN   CHAIN OF LOVE ♪

A Favorite Photo

Memories from the Year of _____

OUR
TRADITIONS

GETTING THE TREE, VISITING, HOLIDAY BAKING, HANGING THE STOCKINGS, EGGNOG

_____

_____

_____

_____

_____

Memories are made of this ❤ _____

_____

_____

_____

_____

_____

_____

_____

_____

Our Favorite Christmas

Decorations _____ ♪

Ornaments _____

Carols _____

Food _____

_____

Drink _____

Smell _____

Book _____

_____

Music _____

Movie _____

_____

Moments _____

_____

_____

_____

_____

Best Cookie: _____

_____

Biggest Cookie Monster
THE AWARD GOES TO

_____

Decking the Halls

How we decorated . . . inside & out . . .

. . . ♫ OH, THE WEATHER OUTSIDE ♪ IS FRIGHTFUL,

BUT ♫ THE FIRE IS SO DELIGHTFUL ♪ . . .

The Tree

How dear the memory is to me,
The lights, the fun,
the Christmas tree. ♥

Dear Santa,

We've been soooo good ♡. We hope you'll bring us . . .

HO HO HO

CHRISTMAS IS FOR CHILDREN

PLACE A PHOTO HERE, DEAR.

His eyes how they twinkled!
His dimples how merry!
His cheeks were like roses,
His nose like a cherry!

Noticing the
Little Things...

_____
_____
_____
_____

Something Funny
Happened...

CHRISTMAS BLOOPERS & PRACTICAL JOKES
_____
_____
_____
_____

WHAT FUN IT IS TO LAUGH & SING...

_____
_____

HOW'S THE WEATHER?

It's that time of year when
it's good to be
fat & jolly ♥

OH BY GOSH BY GOLLY

Favorite
Parties...
_____
_____
_____
_____
_____
CELEBRATIONS _____
_____
_____
_____

Festivities _____
_____
_____
_____

TIME FOR MISTLETOE & HOLLY

Our Friends

"The simplest pleasures warm true friends most easily." *Alyson Roay*

PHOTO HERE

A loving heart is the truest wisdom.
♡ CHARLES DICKENS

MISTLETOE KISSES

A JOY SHARED IS A JOY DOUBLED

The whole family has to sign their names — tell a joke, a story; tell about their favorite things; the family pet, new faces in the family — people we miss, places we love to go, how we share our good fortune.

"For somehow, not only at Christmas, but all the long year through, the joy that you give to others is the joy that comes back to you."
♥ John Greenleaf Whittier

MERRY CHRISTMAS

Christmas Eve

Table, menu, guests, toasts, music, last~minute wrapping...

Snacks for Santa

'Twas The Night Before Christmas...

OH BY GOSH BY JINGLE

Darkness Falls Stars Appear
Evening Angels Gather Here

SWEET DREAMS

Backward, turn backward,
O Time in your flight;
Make me a child again
Just for tonight. ♥ Elizabeth Akers Allen

UNDER THE TREE

NO PEEKING

SHHHH

Best-Kept Secret . . .

The best gifts are tied with
heartstrings.

MERRY CHRISTMAS

On Christmas Day...

HO HO HO

I heard the bells
on Christmas Day
The old familiar
carols play
of Peace on Earth
Good will to All.

Christmas Dinner
Guests • Menu • Flowers

_____

_____

_____

_____

_____

_____

_____

_____

_____

_____

Our Christmas Prayer _____

_____

_____

_____

Every act of love
is a work of peace
no matter how small.
♥ Mother Teresa

HOME for CHRISTMAS

BLESSINGS

THERE'S NO PLACE LIKE H♥ME

HAPPY
NEW YEAR

TO US

RING OUT THE OLD, RING IN THE NEW

We Brought in the New Year. . . .

AND CELEBRATED NEW YEAR'S DAY. . .

"**L**ost, yesterday, somewhere between sunrise and sunset, two golden hours, each set with sixty diamond minutes. No reward is offered, for they are gone forever."

♥ Horace Mann

We resolve...

★

★

★

★

★

★

★

★

★

Before you go to bed on December 31st, join hands, say a prayer, & make a wish for the coming year. It's been proven that, when lots of people pray at the same time, miracles can happen. "In this season it is well to reassert that the hope of mankind rests in faith. Believing there is hope for the world is a way to move toward it." ♥ Gladys Taber

FAITH

Glue your family
Christmas card,
your dinner menu,
or favorite party
invitation here.

CHRISTMAS STAMP

Glue
Here

OUR FAMILY
GOD BLESS US EVERY ONE

CHAIN - CHAIN - CHAIN   CHAIN OF LOVE ♪

A Favorite Photo

Memories from the Year of _____

OUR
TRADITIONS

GETTING THE TREE, VISITING, HOLIDAY BAKING, HANGING THE STOCKINGS, EGGNOG

_____

_____

_____

_____

_____

_____

Memories are made of this ♥ _____

_____

_____

_____

_____

_____

_____

_____

_____

_____

Our Favorite Christmas

Decorations _____ ♪

Ornaments 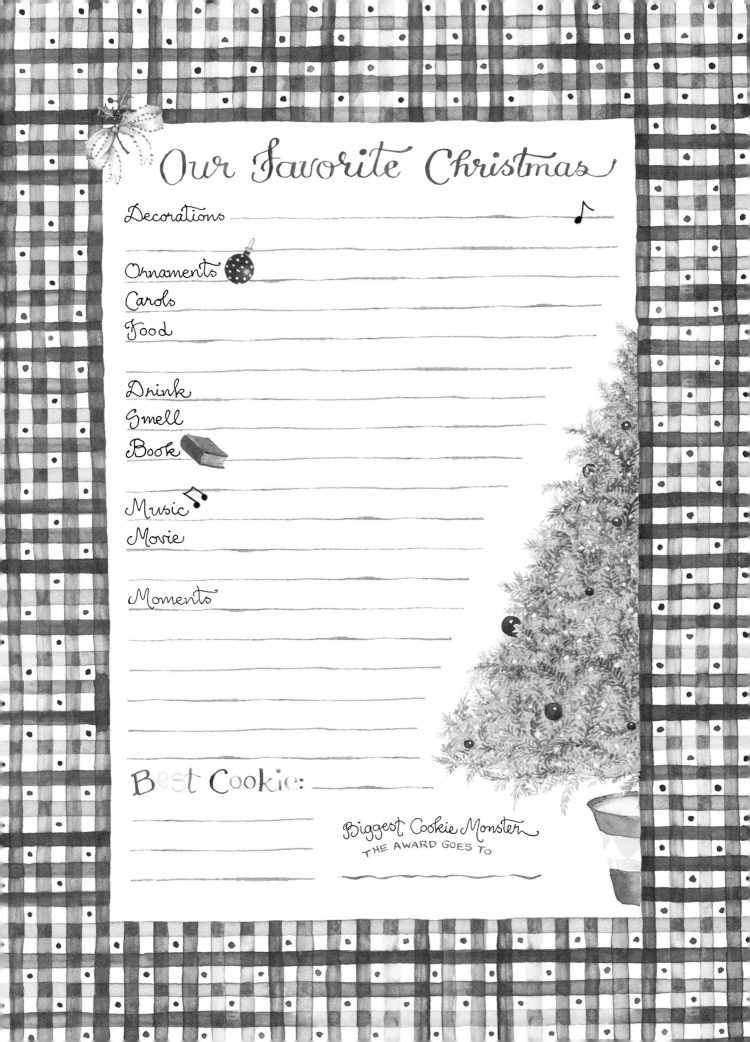 _____

Carols _____

Food _____

_____

Drink _____

Smell _____

Book _____

_____

Music ♫ _____

Movie _____

_____

Moments _____

_____

_____

_____

_____

Best Cookie: _____

_____

_____

Biggest Cookie Monster
THE AWARD GOES TO

_____

Decking the Halls

How we decorated . . . . inside & out . . .

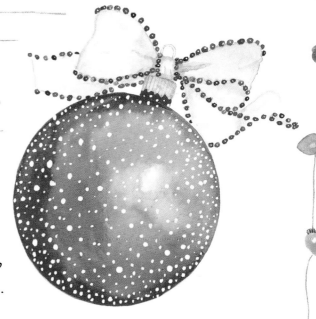

. . . ♪ OH, THE WEATHER OUTSIDE ♪ IS FRIGHTFUL,

BUT ♫ THE FIRE IS SO DELIGHTFUL ♪ . . .

The Tree

How dear the memory is to me,
The lights, the fun,
the Christmas tree. ♥

Dear Santa,

We've been soooo good 💙. We hope you'll bring us . . .

HO HO HO

CHRISTMAS IS FOR CHILDREN

PLACE A PHOTO HERE,
DEAR.

His eyes how they twinkled!
His dimples how merry!
His cheeks were like roses,
His nose like a cherry!

Noticing the
Little Things...

_____
_____
_____
_____

Something Funny
Happened...

CHRISTMAS BLOOPERS & PRACTICAL JOKES
_____
_____
_____
_____

♪ WHAT FUN IT IS TO LAUGH & SING... ♫

_____
_____
_____

HOW'S THE WEATHER?
_____
_____

It's that time of year when
it's good to be
fat & jolly ♡

OH BY GOSH BY GOLLY

Favorite
Parties...
_____
_____
_____
_____
_____
_____ CELEBRATIONS _____
_____
_____
Festivities _____
_____
_____
_____

TIME FOR MISTLETOE & HOLLY

Our Friends

"The simplest pleasures warm true friends most easily." *Alyson Roay*

PHOTO
HERE

A loving heart is the truest wisdom.
♥ CHARLES DICKENS

A JOY SHARED IS A JOY DOUBLED

The whole family has to sign their names — tell a joke, a story; tell about their favorite things; the family pet, new faces in the family — people we miss, places we love to go, how we share our good fortune.

"For somehow, not only at Christmas, but all the long
year through, the joy that you give to others is
the joy that comes back to you."
♥ John Greenleaf Whittier

MERRY CHRISTMAS

Christmas Eve

Table, menu, guests, toasts, music, last~minute wrapping...

Snacks for Santa

'Twas The Night Before Christmas...

OH BY GOSH BY JINGLE

DARKNESS FALLS STARS APPEAR
EVENING ANGELS GATHER HERE

SWEET DREAMS

Backward, turn backward,
O Time in your flight;
Make me a child again
Just for tonight. ♥ Elizabeth Akers Allen

Under the Tree

NO PEEKING

SHHHH

Best-Kept Secret...

The best gifts are tied with heartstrings.

MERRY CHRISTMAS

On Christmas Day...

HO HO HO

I heard the bells
on Christmas Day
The old familiar
carols play
of Peace on Earth
Good will to All.

Christmas Dinner
Guests • Menu • Flowers

_____

_____

_____

_____

_____

_____

_____

_____

_____

Our Christmas Prayer _____

_____

_____

Every act of love
is a work of peace
no matter how small.
♥ Mother Teresa

HOME for CHRISTMAS

BLESSINGS

THERE'S NO PLACE LIKE H♥ME

HAPPY NEW YEAR

To Us

RING OUT THE OLD, RING IN THE NEW

We Brought in the New Year....

AND CELEBRATED NEW YEAR'S DAY...

"**L**ost, yesterday, somewhere between sunrise and sunset, two golden hours, each set with sixty diamond minutes. No reward is offered, for they are gone forever."

♥ Horace Mann

We resolve...

★

★

★

★

★

★

★

★

★

Before you go to bed on December 31st, join hands, say a prayer, & make a wish for the coming year. It's been proven that; when lots of people pray at the same time, miracles can happen. "In this season it is well to reassert that the hope of mankind rests in faith. Believing there is hope for the world is a way to move toward it." ♥ Gladys Taber

FAITH

Glue your family
Christmas card,
your dinner menu,
or favorite party
invitation here.

CHRISTMAS STAMP

Glue
Here

OUR FAMILY

GOD BLESS US EVERY ONE

CHAIN — CHAIN — CHAIN   CHAIN OF LOVE ♪

A Favorite Photo

Memories from the Year of _____

OUR TRADITIONS

GETTING THE TREE, VISITING, HOLIDAY BAKING, HANGING THE STOCKINGS, EGGNOG

_____

_____

_____

_____

_____

_____

Memories are made of this ♥ _____

_____

_____

_____

_____

_____

_____

_____

_____

_____

Our Favorite Christmas

Decorations _____

Ornaments _____

Carols _____

Food _____

Drink _____

Smell _____

Book _____

Music _____

Movie _____

Moments _____

Best Cookie: _____

Biggest Cookie Monster
THE AWARD GOES TO

Decking the Halls

How we decorated . . . . inside & out . . .

_____

_____

_____

_____

_____

_____

_____

_____

_____

_____

_____

_____

_____

_____

_____

_____

_____

. . . ♫ OH, THE WEATHER OUTSIDE ♪ IS FRIGHTFUL,

BUT ♫ THE FIRE IS SO DELIGHTFUL ♪ . . .

The Tree

How dear the memory is to me,
The lights, the fun,
the Christmas tree. ♥

Dear Santa,

We've been soooo good ♥. We hope you'll bring us . . .

HO HO HO

CHRISTMAS IS FOR CHILDREN

PLACE A PHOTO HERE,
DEAR.

His eyes how they twinkled!
His dimples how merry!
His cheeks were like roses,
His nose like a cherry!

Noticing the
Little Things...

Something Funny
Happened...

CHRISTMAS BLOOPERS & PRACTICAL JOKES

♪ WHAT FUN IT IS TO LAUGH & SING... ♪

HOW'S THE WEATHER?

It's that time of year when
it's good to be
fat & jolly ♥

OH BY GOSH BY GOLLY

Favorite
Parties...

CELEBRATIONS

Festivities

TIME FOR MISTLETOE & HOLLY

Our Friends

"The simplest pleasures warm true friends most easily." *Alyson Roay*

PHOTO
HERE

A loving heart is the truest wisdom.
♥ CHARLES DICKENS

MISTLETOE KISSES

A JOY SHARED IS A JOY DOUBLED

The whole family has to sign their names — tell a joke, a story; tell about their favorite things; the family pet, new faces in the family — people we miss, places we love to go, how we share our good fortune.

"For somehow, not only at Christmas, but all the long year through, the joy that you give to others is the joy that comes back to you."

John Greenleaf Whittier

MERRY CHRISTMAS

Christmas Eve

Table, menu, guests, toasts, music, last~minute wrapping...

Snacks for Santa

'Twas The Night Before Christmas...

OH BY GOSH BY JINGLE

Darkness Falls Stars Appear
Evening Angels Gather Here

TIME FOR PRESENTS & KRIS KRINGLE

SWEET DREAMS

Backward, turn backward,
O Time in your flight;
Make me a child again
Just for tonight. ♥ Elizabeth Akers Allen

UNDER THE TREE

NO PEEKING

SHHHH

Best-Kept Secret...

The best gifts are tied with heartstrings.

MERRY CHRISTMAS

On Christmas Day...

HoHoHo

I heard the bells
on Christmas Day
The old familiar
carols play
of Peace on Earth
Good will to All.

Christmas Dinner

Guests · Menu · Flowers

Our Christmas Prayer

Every act of love
is a work of peace
no matter how small.
♥ Mother Teresa

HOME for CHRISTMAS

BLESSINGS

THERE'S NO PLACE LIKE H♥ME

To Us

HAPPY
NEW YEAR

RING OUT THE OLD, RING IN THE NEW

We Brought in the New Year . . . .

AND CELEBRATED NEW YEAR'S DAY . . .

"**L**ost, yesterday, somewhere between sunrise and sunset, two golden hours, each set with sixty diamond minutes. No reward is offered, for they are gone forever."

♥ Horace Mann

We resolve...

★

★

★

★

★

★

★

★

★

Before you go to bed on December 31st, join hands, say a prayer, & make a wish for the coming year. It's been proven that, when lots of people pray at the same time, miracles can happen. "In this season it is well to reassert that the hope of mankind rests in faith. Believing there is hope for the world is a way to move toward it." ♥ Gladys Taber

FAITH

Glue your family
Christmas card,
your dinner menu,
or favorite party
invitation here.

CHRISTMAS STAMP

Glue
Here

OUR FAMILY

GOD BLESS US EVERY ONE

CHAIN-CHAIN-CHAIN   CHAIN OF LOVE ♪

A Favorite Photo

Memories from the Year of _____

OUR
TRADITIONS

GETTING THE TREE, VISITING, HOLIDAY BAKING, HANGING THE STOCKINGS, EGGNOG

_____
_____
_____
_____
_____
_____

Memories are made of this ♥ _____
_____
_____
_____
_____
_____
_____
_____
_____
_____
_____

Our Favorite Christmas

Decorations _____

_____

Ornaments _____

Carols _____

Food _____

_____

Drink _____

Smell _____

Book _____

_____

Music _____

Movie _____

_____

Moments _____

_____

_____

_____

Best Cookie: _____

_____

Biggest Cookie Monster
THE AWARD GOES TO

_____

Decking the Halls

How we decorated . . . inside & out . . .

_____

_____

_____

_____

_____

_____

_____

_____

_____

_____

_____

_____

_____

_____

_____

_____

_____

_____

. . .♫ OH, THE WEATHER OUTSIDE ♪ IS FRIGHTFUL,

BUT ♫ THE FIRE IS SO DELIGHTFUL ♪. . .

The Tree

How dear the memory is to me,
The lights, the fun,
the Christmas tree. ♥

Dear Santa,

We've been soooo good ♥. We hope you'll bring us . . .

HO HO HO

CHRISTMAS IS FOR CHILDREN

PLACE A PHOTO HERE, DEAR.

His eyes how they twinkled!
His dimples how merry!
His cheeks were like roses,
His nose like a cherry!

Noticing the Little Things...

_____
_____
_____
_____

Something Funny Happened...

CHRISTMAS BLOOPERS & PRACTICAL JOKES
_____
_____
_____
_____

WHAT FUN IT IS TO LAUGH & SING...

_____
_____

HOW'S THE WEATHER?
_____
_____

It's that time of year when it's good to be fat & jolly ♥

OH BY GOSH BY GOLLY

Favorite
Parties...
_____

_____

_____

_____

CELEBRATIONS

_____

_____

_____

Festivities
_____

_____

_____

TIME FOR MISTLETOE & HOLLY

Our Friends

"The simplest pleasures warm true friends most easily." *Alyson Roay*

PHOTO
HERE

A loving heart is the truest wisdom.
♡ CHARLES DICKENS

MISTLETOE KISSES

A JOY SHARED IS A JOY DOUBLED

The whole family has to a story; tell about their new faces in the family love to go, how we share sign their names — tell a joke, favorite things; the family pet, — people we miss, places we our good fortune.

_____

_____

_____

_____

_____

_____

_____

_____

_____

_____

_____

_____

_____

_____

_____

_____

"For somehow, not only at Christmas, but all the long year through, the joy that you give to others is the joy that comes back to you."

♥ John Greenleaf Whittier

MERRY CHRISTMAS

Christmas Eve

Table, menu, guests, toasts,   music, last~minute wrapping...

Snacks for Santa

'Twas The Night Before Christmas...

OH BY GOSH BY JINGLE

DARKNESS FALLS STARS APPEAR
EVENING ANGELS GATHER HERE

SWEET DREAMS

TIME FOR PRESENTS & KRIS KRINGLE

Backward, turn backward,
O Time in your flight;
Make me a child again
Just for tonight. ♥ Elizabeth Akers Allen

Under the Tree

joy

NO PEEKING

SHHHH

Best-Kept Secret . . .

The best gifts are tied with heartstrings.

MERRY CHRISTMAS

On Christmas Day...

I heard the bells
on Christmas Day
The old familiar
carols play
Peace on Earth
Good will to All.

Christmas Dinner
Guests · Menu · Flowers

_____

_____

_____

_____

_____

_____

_____

_____

_____

Our Christmas Prayer _____

_____

_____

Every act of love
is a work of peace
no matter how small.
♥ Mother Teresa

HOME for CHRISTMAS

BLESSINGS

THERE'S NO PLACE LIKE HOME

TO US

HAPPY
NEW YEAR

RING OUT THE OLD, RING IN THE NEW

We Brought in the New Year....

AND CELEBRATED NEW YEAR'S DAY...

"**L**ost, yesterday, somewhere between sunrise and sunset, two golden hours, each set with sixty diamond minutes. No reward is offered, for they are gone forever."

♥ Horace Mann

We resolve...

★

★

★

★

★

★

★

★

★

Before you go to bed on December 31st, join hands, say a prayer, & make a wish for the coming year. It's been proven that, when lots of people pray at the same time, miracles can happen. "In this season it is well to reassert that the hope of mankind rests in faith. Believing there is hope for the world is a way to move toward it." ♥ Gladys Taber

FAITH

Memories
are made
of this ♥